CW00382384

This is a work of fiction.
Names, characters, places and incidents either are
the product of the author's imagination
or are used fictitiously.

ISBN: 9798592645877

First Edition April 2021

Little girl wanders: A volunteer vacation

Little girl wanders: A volunteer vacation

Written by : Eleni Charalambous
Illustrated by: Tanja Varcelija

This book belongs to:

____

____

who will always help others.

To all of those who give up their free time to make a difference.

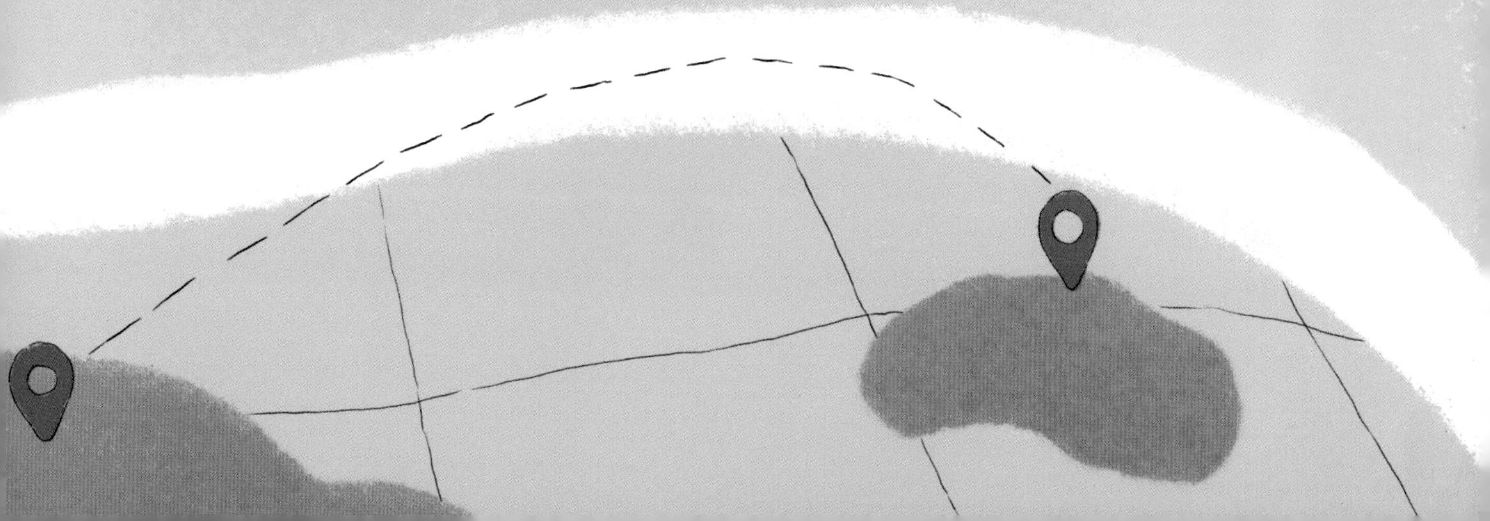

I always knew I would volunteer,
I wanted to go and make some things very clear.
That, wherever we go and whatever we do,
the people we help will always be part of you!

So, when I was older, I packed my bags
and decided for a life that didn't involve tags.
I chose some countries that needed help,
and booked flights for those whose lack of support I felt.

So, I went to Bali to teach their youth.
It was hot and humid but gave me proof
that everyone, everywhere, are all the same -
even if they can't pronounce your name.

I went to Greece to help the community and guess what?
They were just like you and me!
They ate,
they drank
and they played outside.

The language was different
but that was no reason to divide.

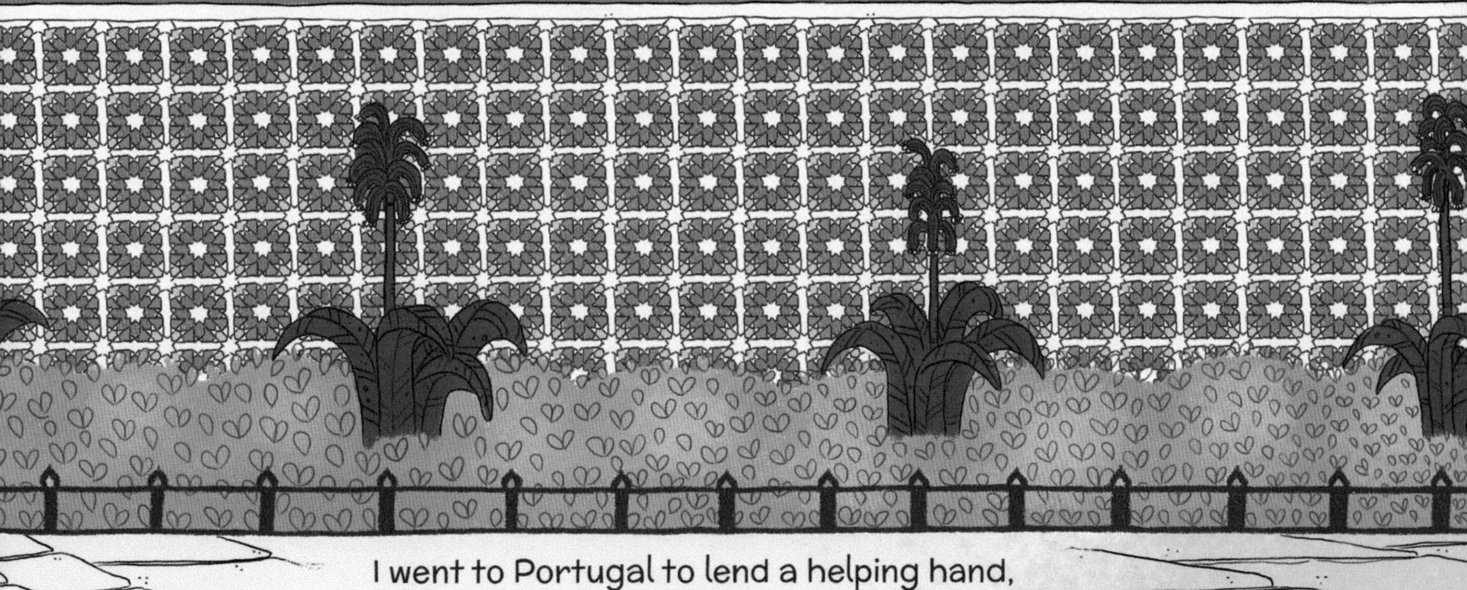

I went to Portugal to lend a helping hand,
there were children playing all over the land.
The culture was vibrant, and their food delicious,
they treated me so kindly; giving me so many kind wishes.

I went to Africa to teach in a school,
they enjoyed every day, that was their main rule.
They ran, they jumped, they laughed and they cried.
It showed me that we are all the same, inside.

I went to China to give them my support,
it was a lot more powerful than I thought.

I helped with the pandas and preparing food,
it always put me in such a good mood.

I was helping and they were glad,
it prevented many animals and humans from being sad!

I have learnt that volunteering is a powerful tool
and can be done by everyone, before, during and after school.
There are no limitations, there are no rules,
all it takes is your free time, a smile ....
and it is so much cooler than sitting by a pool.

Every country, every place,
there is no right or wrong race.
We all have feelings, families and love,
and we all look at the same stars above.

Eleni, British born with love for all things rhyming,
written and pun-related.

She gained a BA in Fashion Journalism in 2010 in
London where her love for writing continued to blossom.

She continued her education by travelling
to Greece in 2016 where she became TEFL certified.

She has since travelled to multiple countries
volunteering and teaching
English to children around the world, which has consequently
led to her inspiration for writing poems for children.

Always looks for the good in everyone
and always believes tomorrow will be better.

For my Father who always taught me the art of being helpful.

For my Mother who taught me the art of being kind.

For my partner who took me on an inspirational vacation.

For Katinka, who has been reading my work since 2001.

For everyone who puts their voice into action and volunteers.

How Can I Change the World?

leniwrites

leniwritesbooks

leniwrites.com

Eleni Charalambous

Printed in Great Britain
by Amazon